I BELIEVE in YOU!

sourcebooks
jabberwocky

Marianne Richmond

You came into the WORLD with a

SPECIAL JOB

to do, the one of GROWING UP into

The BEST and BRIGHTEST you!

Some days,
it's SMOOTH
and EASY.

And others?
ROUGH
and TOUGH.

Monday's "BRING IT ON!"
turns into Friday's
"HaD ENouGH!"

Whether SUN
or RAIN or IN-BETWEEN,
one thing is

Always
True.

I'M HERE
to cheer you onward,
because

I BELIEVE in YOU!

When your project feels **TOO HARD,** and you want to go to bed,

I believe in your

SMART THINKING

to TRY and

LEARN instead.

When the TEAM YOU LIKE says,

"No, some other kid will play,"

I BELIEVE in your
AWESOME SKILLS
to SHINE a different way!

When the MONSTERS
in your mind seem

TOO
BiG

to fight yourself,

I believe in your **DEEP COURAGE** to reach out and

ASK FOR HELP!

When you

MaKE

a BIG MISTAKE or you

CHOOSE

a hurtful way,

I believe in your

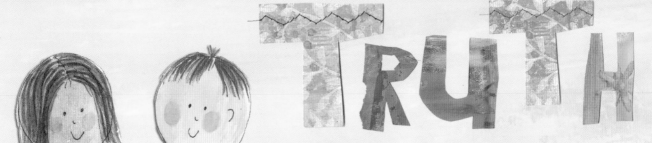

STAND-UP
TRUTH

to say what
YOU SHOULD SAY.

When the day dips

UP
aND
DOWN

like a
roller coaster ride,

I believe in your

GREAT ATTITUDE

to trust the
LOWS and HIGHS.

When you **LOOK**

into the mirror and question

WHO YOU SEE,

I believe in your **TRUE BRILLIANCE**

that SHINES THROUGH from you to me!

When everyone else

STANDS TALL

looking so SURE
and STRONG,

I believe in your

BRAVE SPIRIT

THAT'S IN YOU
ALL ALONG!

When a good friend is UNKIND
or doesn't want to play with you,

I believe in your

PLAYFUL HEART

to find NEW FRIENDS who do!

When LEARNING something

NEW

makes you want to

STOP

and

FRET,

The job of GROWING UP takes

HARD WORK,

I know.

But each day is an ADVENTURE,

each problem

HeLPS YoU GROW!

And I want you to REMEMBER, I'm here to

WATCH THE RIDE.

I believe in

ONE AMAZING YOU

with ALL MY LOVE and pride!

MARIANNE RICHMOND is a bestselling author and artist who has touched the lives of millions for more than two decades by creating books that celebrate the love of family. Visit her at mariannerichmond.com.

"My books help you share your heart and connect with those you love."

Published by Sourcebooks Jabberwocky, an imprint of Sourcebooks Kids
P.O. Box 4410, Naperville, Illinois 60567-4410
(630) 961-3900
sourcebookskids.com

Library of Congress Cataloguing-in-Publication Data is on file with the publisher.

Source of Production: Leo Paper, Heshen City, Guangdong Province, China
Date of Production: July 2022
Run Number: 5027502

Printed and bound in China.
LEO 10 9 8 7 6 5 4 3 2